The Perfectly Perfect Wish

Lisa Mantchev

Illustrated by Jessica Courtney-Tickle

A Paula Wiseman Book

Simon & Schuster Books for Young Readers

New York   London   Toronto   Sydney   New Delhi

For Luka, who arrived at the perfect time

—L. M.

For Erin and Elsie

—J. C.-T.

SIMON & SCHUSTER BOOKS FOR YOUNG READERS
An imprint of Simon & Schuster Children's Publishing Division
1230 Avenue of the Americas, New York, New York 10020

For information about special discounts for bulk purchases, please contact Simon & Schuster Special Sales at 1-866-506-1949 or business@simonandschuster.com.
The Simon & Schuster Speakers Bureau can bring authors to your live event. For more information or to book an event, contact the Simon & Schuster Speakers Bureau at 1-866-248-3049 or visit our website at www.simonspeakers.com.
Book design by Krista Vossen
The text for this book was set in Sentinel.
The illustrations for this book were rendered in watercolor, and digitally.
Manufactured in China
1219 SCP
2 4 6 8 10 9 7 5 3
Library of Congress Cataloging-in-Publication Data
Title: The perfectly perfect wish / written by Lisa Mantchev ; illustrated by Jessica Courtney-Tickle.
Description: First edition. | New York : Simon & Schuster Books for Young Readers, [2020] | "A Paula Wiseman Book."
| Summary: A young girl has so many choices but only one wish.
Identifiers: LCCN 2019006400| ISBN 9781534406193 (hardcover) | ISBN 9781534406209 (eBook)
Subjects: | CYAC: Wishes—Fiction.
Classification: LCC PZ7.M31827 Pe 2020 | DDC [E]—dc23
LC record available at https://lccn.loc.gov/2019006400

Waiting for the school bus, I find
something in the grass.

At first I think it's a marble or a penny or a
four-leaf clover, but marbles and pennies
and clovers are just ordinary things.

And *this* is an *extraordinary* thing.
An extraordinary thing with just one rule:
NO WISHING FOR MORE WISHES.

Which means this is exactly one wish.
No more, no less.

"I found a wish in the grass," I tell Susan the bus driver.
"Just one?" she asks, closing the door with a *clang*!
"Just the one," I answer.

"Think hard, then," she says. "It will need to be
a perfectly perfect wish."

I put the wish in my pocket and wonder what
my perfectly perfect wish should be.
I am still wondering as I sit down next to Eliza.

A blue ribbon at the horse show.

A trip to Japan.

Real ballerina pointe shoes.

So many choices, but only one wish!

"What would you wish for, if you had a
perfectly perfect wish?" I ask Eliza.

She knows right away. "Whenever I see a shooting star, I close my eyes and wish for a puppy."

I nod, because a puppy is always fun, but we already have two dogs *and* a cat.

"What would you wish for, if you had a perfectly
perfect wish?" I ask Mrs. Shue.

She thinks about it for a moment.
"When I pick dandelions and blow all
the seeds away, I wish for a little house
for me and my family."

I nod, because my family has a very nice
house. I even have my own room, with
bunk beds for sleepovers.

"What would you wish for, if you had a perfectly perfect wish?" I ask Mark in the lunch line.

"When I blow out my birthday candles, I wish my daddy would come home safe," he says.

I nod, because I don't have to worry a big worry like that. My daddy is a dentist. He goes to work in the morning and comes back every night.

While I eat my lunch, I think about
winning a blue ribbon at the horse show.

While I run on the playground, I think about a trip to Japan.

Getting on the bus to go home, I think about real ballerina pointe shoes.

I *want* real ballerina pointe shoes now, but Ms. Bartholomew
says not until I am ten, when my toes are strong enough.

I *want* to go to Japan, but I could save up for it.

I *want* a blue ribbon at the horse show,
but not just because I wished for it.

It's harder than I thought it would be, to think of
a perfectly perfect wish.

When I think about Eliza's puppy, and
Mrs. Shue's house, and Mark's daddy,
all of my own wishes feel too small.

So maybe . . .

I wish that everyone's wish comes true.

I finally found my perfectly
perfect wish.